The Sea Shells

S IT FELL TO EARTH AND TRANSFORMED INTO

OF THE

SANDS

Fig. 2. The star hits the ocean.

Fig. 4. The star is now the Island of the Sleepy Sands.

A Mermaid

Sandy

A Great Sea Turtle

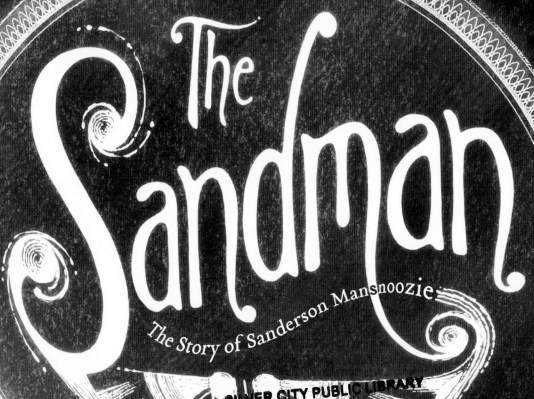

The Sandman

The Story of Sanderson Mansnoozie

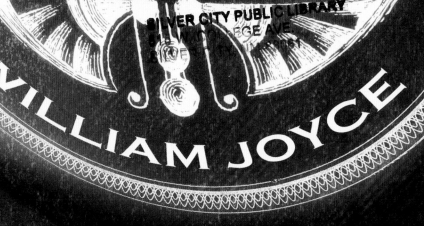

WILLIAM JOYCE

atheneum

Atheneum Books for Young Readers

New York London Toronto Sydney New Delhi

Of course you know the Guardians of Childhood.

You've known them since before you can remember, and you'll know them till your memories are like twilight. The very first guardian was the Man in the Moon, and it was he who found the others.

The Man in the Moon watches over the children of Earth. Like a giant nightlight in the sky, he keeps nightmares away. But when the moon is less than full and bright, who will keep the children safe at night?

The Man in the Moon needed another to help him, so he searched with his telescopes until he saw a face he recognized. He looked once. He looked twice. Could it be? Why, yes, it was the same fellow he'd once sent a wish to, many once upon a times ago. Back when the Man in the Moon was just a very small boy. Back in a time called the Golden Age.

The sleepy little fellow's name was Sanderson Mansnoozie. You may know him better as the Sandman. But he began his journey as just plain Sandy, and this is how he came to be.

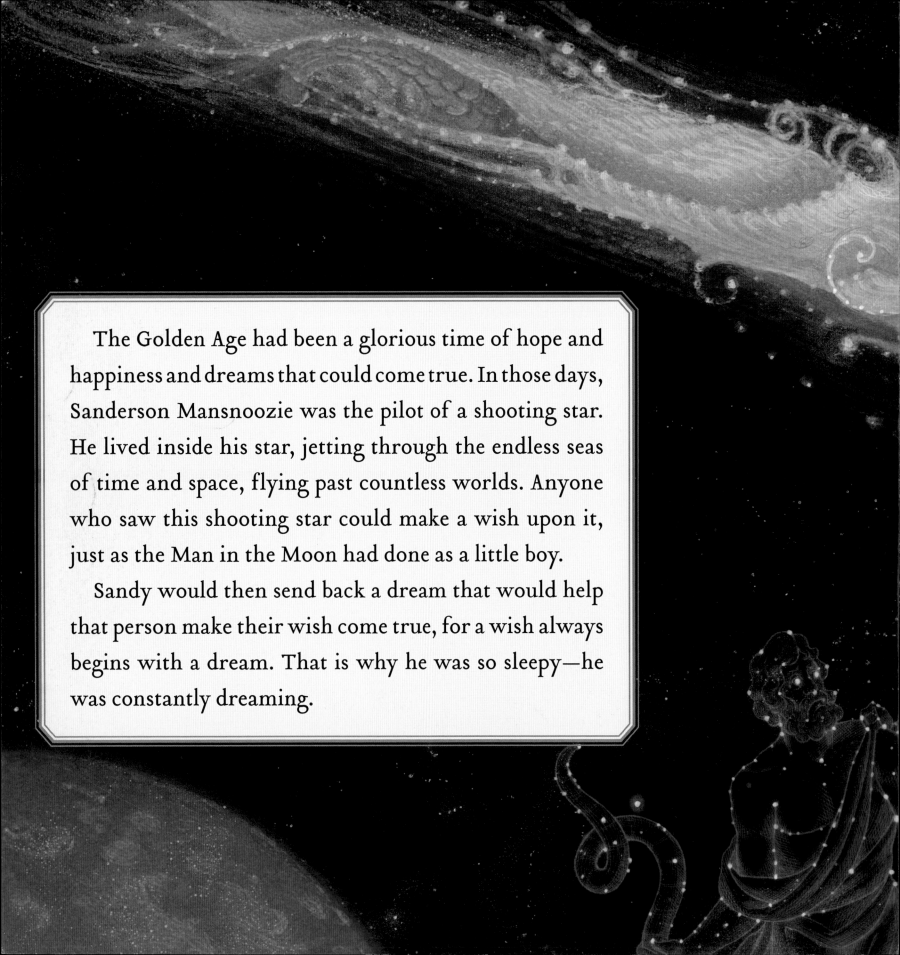

The Golden Age had been a glorious time of hope and happiness and dreams that could come true. In those days, Sanderson Mansnoozie was the pilot of a shooting star. He lived inside his star, jetting through the endless seas of time and space, flying past countless worlds. Anyone who saw this shooting star could make a wish upon it, just as the Man in the Moon had done as a little boy.

Sandy would then send back a dream that would help that person make their wish come true, for a wish always begins with a dream. That is why he was so sleepy—he was constantly dreaming.

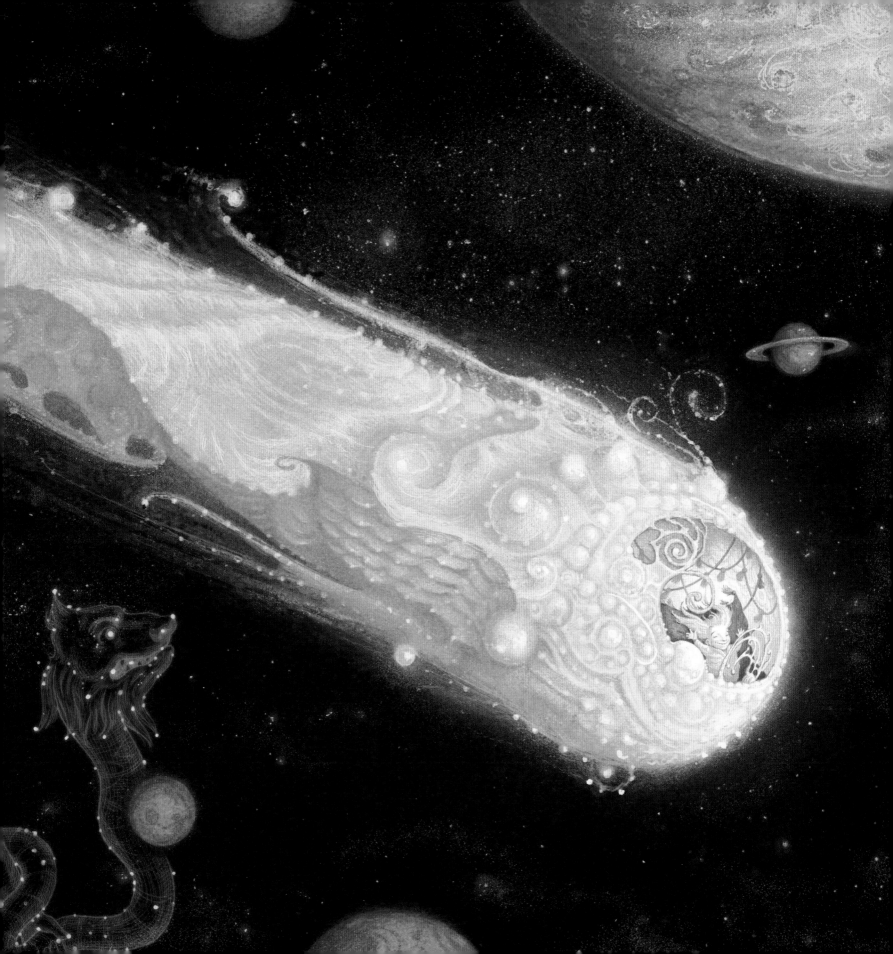

But in this Golden Age, there was one who could not abide anything good or kind or gentle: Pitch, the King of the Nightmares. He had sworn to destroy sweet dreams and shooting stars, and one by one he hunted them down. Sailing in his *Nightmare Galleon* with his Dream Pirates, he would harpoon the stars and drag them to their doom, hurling them into moons, planets, or even the endless darkness of a black hole.

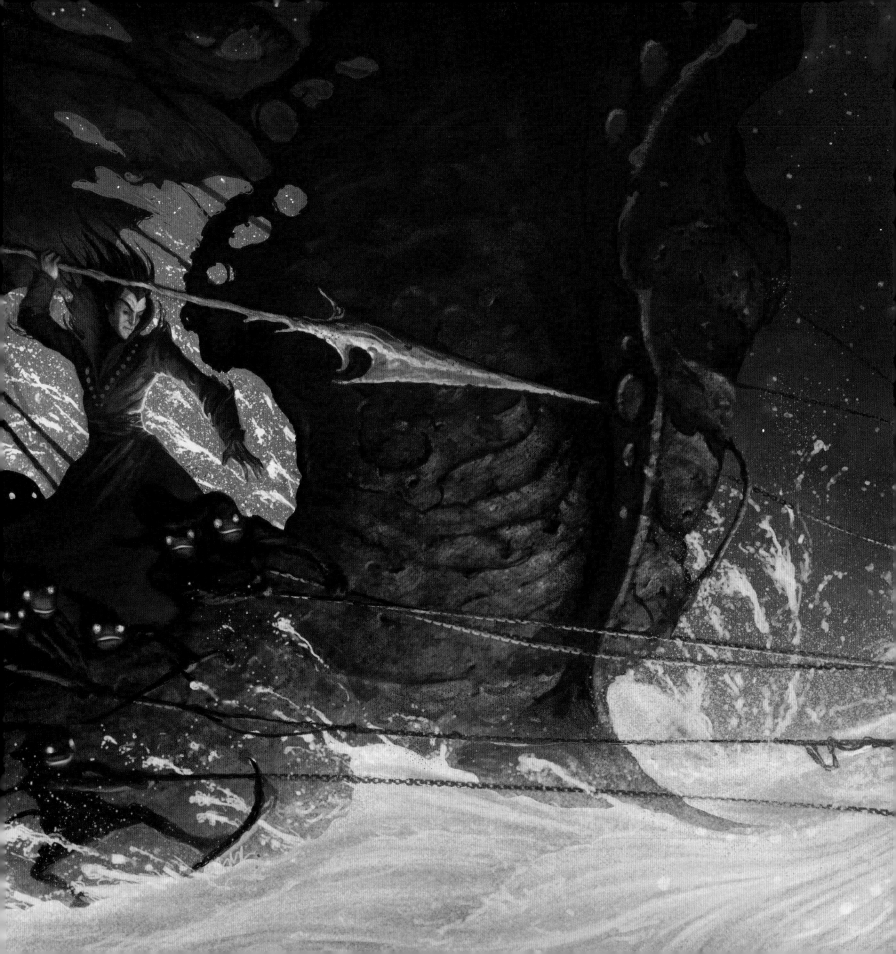

And so it was with Sanderson Mansnoozie and his star. They were near the shoulder of the constellation Orion when Pitch attacked. The Nightmare King lanced the star with his harpoons. For the first time, Sandy knew fear, and his fear only made Pitch stronger. Sandy could not let his star be harmed. He swerved and breached with astonishing daring and finally broke free.

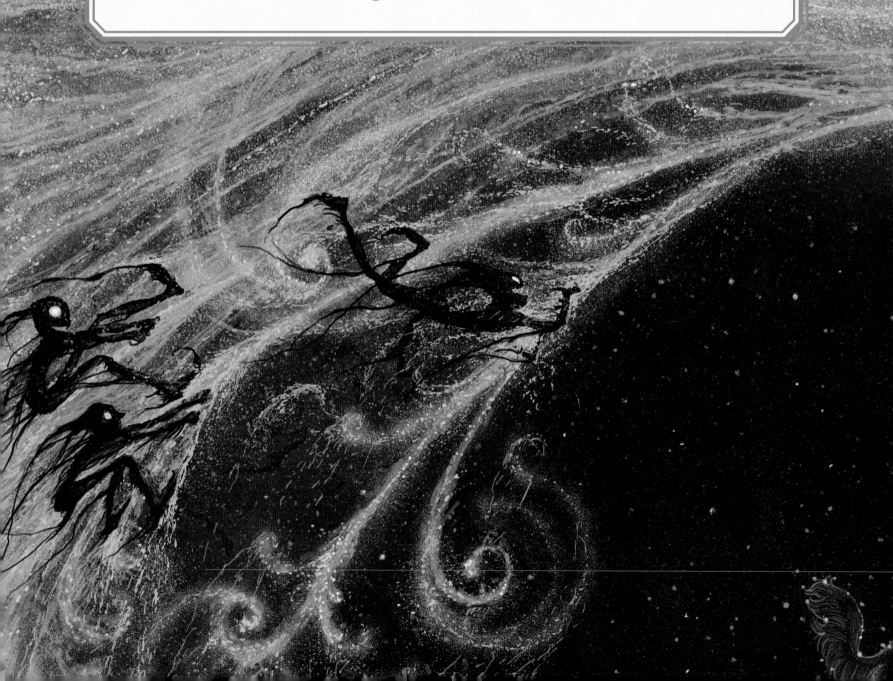

But he lost control of his star. It streaked through space like a missile, a bullet, a wayward arrow of flame and hope.

They tumbled toward a small green and blue planet called Earth. He was certain he would crash. He could hear the laughter of the Dream Pirates, and felt helpless and afraid.

But as Sandy plummeted Earthward, he heard a thousand wishes—the wishes of children, who saw his star streaking toward them. Sandy knew he must not harm a single child, so with all his strength he guided his star away from land and over a vast sea.

Just as he was about to crash, he heard a wish that seemed to come from far, far away. It was bright and clear and kind.

"I wish you well" was all it said.

So Sandy closed his eyes and dreamed that all would be well.

Moments later they crashed into the ocean. The sky was filled with the blinding light of their impact. Then the light faded. The star had neither sunk nor exploded. It had become a sandy sort of island, with long spiraling tendrils of land. At its center were a number of steep dunes, and at the center of the dunes lay Sanderson Mansnoozie.

Above his head, sand was swirling into shapes that were peaceful and soothing.

The faraway wish had been granted. Sanderson Mansnoozie was well, and smiling, and fast asleep.

From all around came the creatures of the sea.

The mermaids were enthralled by Sandy's Dreamsand. And from that moment on they were determined to help this little lost man, a fellow traveler, but from the ocean of the sky.

On and on Sandy slept. And on and on he dreamed. Until every grain of sand on his island contained a dream. Ten thousand nights and dreams passed. Pitch had vanished and so had the Golden Age. The world changed. The island changed. And Sandy changed.

Then one night a moonbeam shined down on him, and he heard the voice from long ago that had wished him well.

"I wish that you would help," said the voice. With that, Sanderson Mansnoozie finally awoke.

There in the moonbeam, he could see the Man in the Moon, who asked, "When the moon's not full and bright, would you keep the children safe at night?"

Sandy nodded, for if a wish was made to him, he still felt bound to answer it.

He walked across the island that had been his star.

He thought and he thought, and he wondered and he wondered. How could he help the children of Earth?

The sea turtles came to him. Some had once belonged to children and knew of their fear of the dark.

The sea shells had more to tell. Countless children had held them to their ears to hear the call of the sea, so the shells had learned their secret joys and sorrows. The sea shells told him that Pitch's Dream Pirates still roamed the night in search of sleeping children to hazard.

Sandy knew that to help the children, he must once again face his ancient enemies. For the second time in his life, he felt afraid.

For days and days, his restless mind would not let him sleep. Without sleep, he had no dreams, and without dreams, he could do nothing.

But the mermaids knew a way to help their friend. They came from the sea with a sweet lullaby. "Dreams, sweet dreams, be in the sand you hold. They banish all the darkling fears and fill the night with gold."

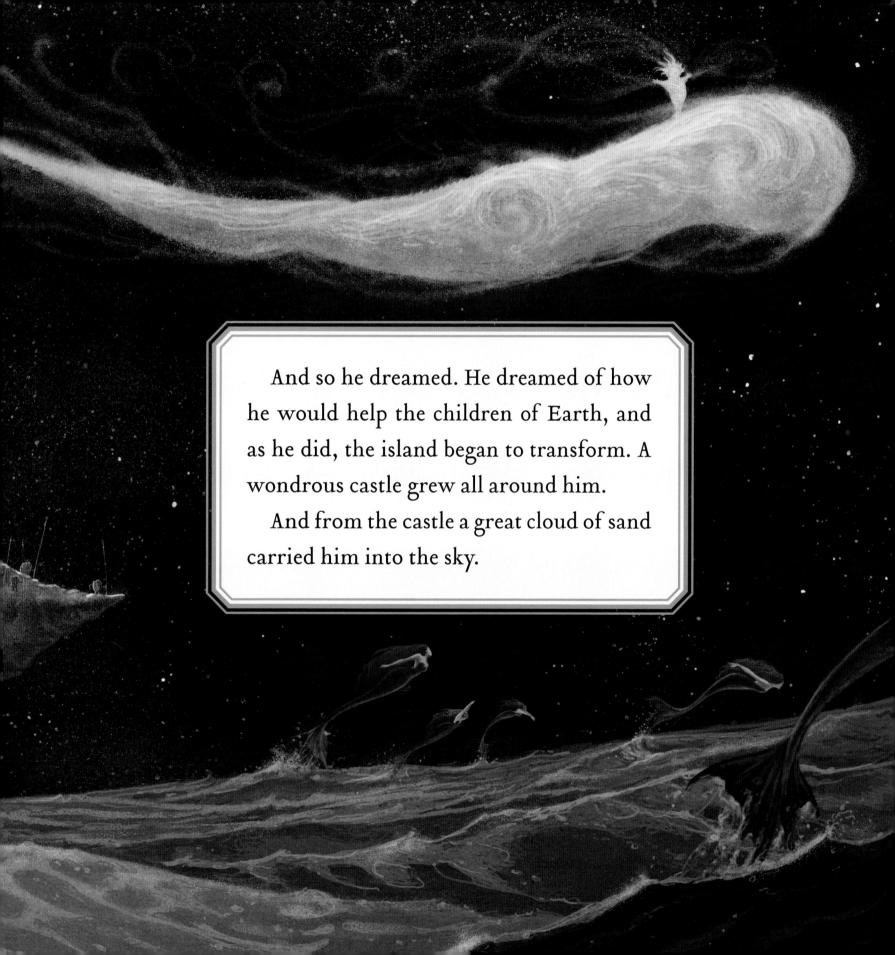

And so he dreamed. He dreamed of how he would help the children of Earth, and as he did, the island began to transform. A wondrous castle grew all around him.

And from the castle a great cloud of sand carried him into the sky.

And on this cloud he journeyed to every land. And to every child who was sleeping, he sent a lovely dream with his Dreamsand. And from every dark corner of the world, the children slept unafraid, for all the nightmares were chased away . . .

. . . chased away by the Dreamsand—chased up to Sandy's cloud. As they came, he grabbed each nightmare and said, "You are not real. You are not true. You are nothing." And as Sandy's fear vanished, so did the nightmares. One by one, they turned harmless—to golden Dreamsand.

And for the first time in all the history of sleep on Earth, there was not a single nightmare to be had.

The moon peeked through the cloudy sky and shined down upon Sanderson Mansnoozie.

"You've granted my wish," the Man in the Moon said to him. "Now I shall grant you a name worthy of your talents." Sandy bowed as the moon declared, "From this moment on you shall be known as His Nocturnal Magnificence, Sanderson Mansnoozie, Sandman the First, Lord High Protector of Sleep and Dreams."

Now the Man in the Moon had his first helper. And from that night on, the Sandman has made his rounds, be the sky cloudy or bright, to send forth his Dreamsand.

ow, most every night is filled with sweet dreams. It's rare for Dreamsand to miss its proper mark, but if it does, a nightmare might try to sneak into your dream. But *you* know it's not real.

So when you've had a good night's sleep and a wonderful dream, you might thank your gentle friend, His Nocturnal Magnificence, Sanderson Mansnoozie, Sandman the First, Lord High Protector of Sleep and Dreams. A longish name to be sure. But worthy of a diligent dreamer who started his journey as just plain Sandy.

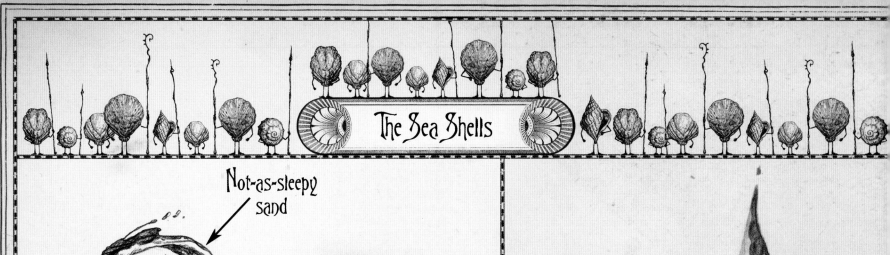

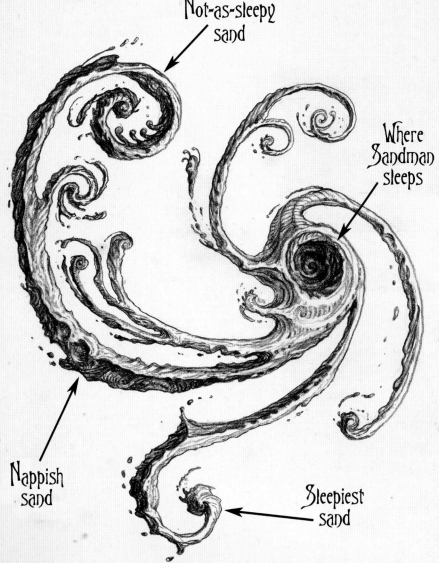

Not-as-sleepy sand

Where Sandman sleeps

Nappish sand

Sleepiest sand

THE ISLAND OF THE
SLEEPY SANDS
(AS VIEWED FROM ABOVE)

THE SHAPE AND SCALE

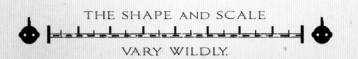

VARY WILDLY.

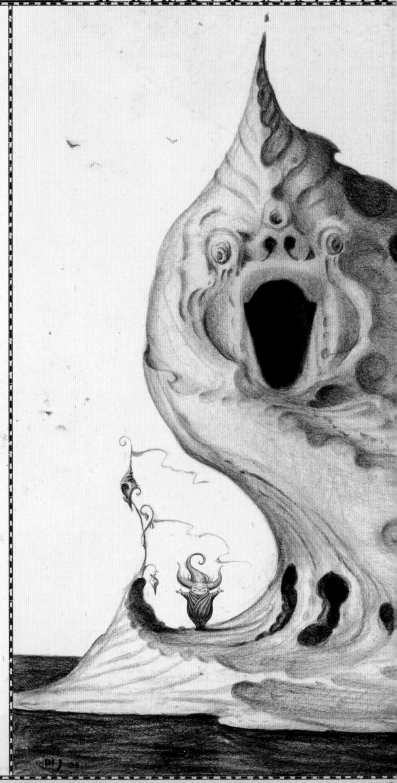